To Catherine, Jean and Joe, my favorite stars.

Book design by Sara Gillingham.
Typeset in Coop Condensed and Gill Sans.
The illustrations in this book were rendered in paper collage.
Printed in Mexico.

Library of Congress Cataloging-in-Publication Data
Barner, Bob. Stars! stars! stars! / by Bob Barner.
p. cm.
Summary: Simple rhyming text describes stars and
the planets of our solar system.
ISBN 0-8118-3159-0
1. Planets—Juvenile literature. 2. Stars—Juvenile literature.
[1.Stars. 2. Planets.]   I.Title.
QB602 .B365 2002
520--dc21
2001004064

Distributed in Canada by Raincoast Books
9050 Shaughnessy Street, Vancouver, British Columbia V6P 6E5

10 9 8 7 6 5 4 3 2 1

Chronicle Books LLC
85 Second Street, San Francisco, California 94105

www.chroniclekids.com

Stars! Stars! Stars!

by Bob Barner

chronicle books · san francisco

Stars! Stars! Stars!

I want to see planets and stars!

Bright stars twinkling above big city lights

Distant planets glowing
over black country nights

Constellations *that take shape*

when I connect them with lines

Milky Way stars shining two hundred billion times

The Sun that burns with golden light

Hot planet **Mercury** turning slowly in the night

Venus, the Evening Star,

first planet to shine
in the twilight sky

Blue-green **Earth** with

the dusty **Moon** orbiting by

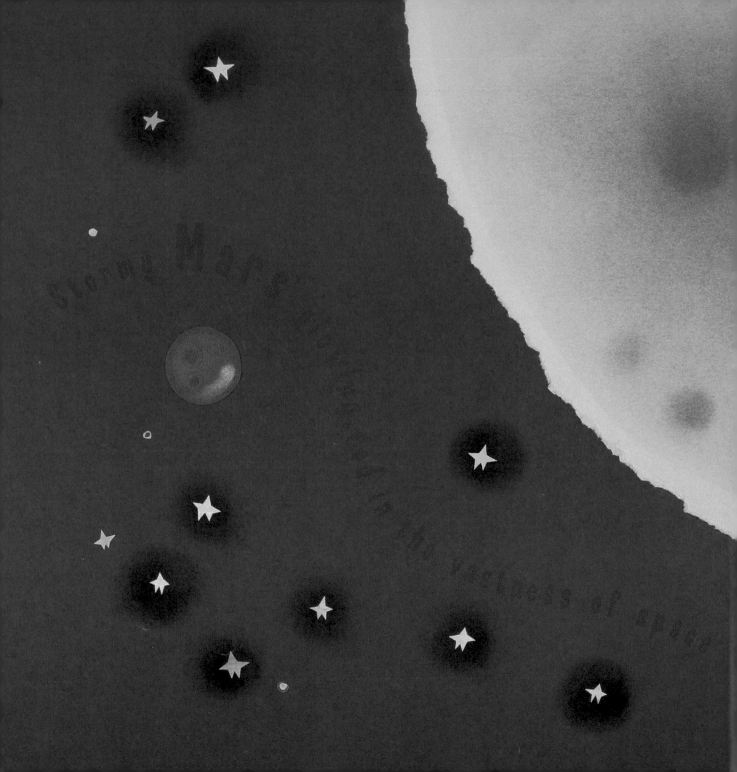

Giant planet Jupiter moving with grace

Saturn circled by rings and

Uranus spinning on its side

Windy Neptune and tiny Pluto orbiting wide

The Big Dipper holding a scoop of night

Stars! Stars! Stars!

I want to see planets and stars tonight!

Meet the Planets!

The Sun is a medium-size star. All nine of the planets in our solar system orbit the Sun. The Sun has been burning for about 5 billion years.

Mercury, the closest planet to the Sun, is only a little larger than the Moon. Its surface is covered with tall mountains and deep craters.

Venus is a planet, but it is called the Evening Star because it is usually the first light we see shining in the evening sky.

Earth, our home, is the only planet in our solar system that we know supports life.

Mars, the red planet, is about half the size of Earth. Mars looks red because it is covered with rust-colored soil.

Jupiter is the largest planet in our solar system. It is so big that all of the other planets could fit inside it.

Saturn is not very dense and would float in water. Its rings are made of pieces of dust and ice varying from as small as a pea to as large as a car.

Uranus spins on its side. The narrow ring around Uranus is made of black ice.

Neptune, the blue planet, has winds that blow up to 1,500 miles per hour (2,420 km/h). Its blue color is caused by methane in its atmosphere.

Pluto, the smallest planet, is smaller than the Moon. Pluto is also farthest from the Sun, as far as 4.6 billion miles (7.38 billion km)!

Meet the
Universe!

A **star** is a giant ball of glowing gas. Stars twinkle because we see them through layers of moving air in Earth's atmosphere.

A **constellation** is a group of stars that people connect with imaginary lines to form a design. There are 88 constellations in the sky.

A **sun** is any star that is the center of a planetary system. Our sun is a medium-size star.

A **planet** is a large object that orbits a sun but doesn't make its own light. Planets reflect the light from stars. They don't twinkle because they are closer to Earth than stars are.

Gravity is the force that keeps objects in orbit. Gravity keeps us from floating off the Earth!

A **moon** orbits a planet the way a planet orbits a sun. Some planets, such as Saturn, have many moons.

An **asteroid** is a rocky object, much smaller than a planet, that orbits a sun.

★

A **comet** is made of ice and dust and orbits a sun.

★

A **meteor** is a space rock that crashes into the surface of a planet or moon.

★

A **shooting star** isn't a star at all. It's a meteor that burns up when it gets close to Earth.

A **solar system** is all of the planets, moons, asteroids, comets and other matter that orbits a sun.

★

A **galaxy** is made up of billions of stars, gas and dust held together by gravity. Planet Earth is in the Milky Way Galaxy.

★

The **universe** is all of the light, matter and energy that exists in time and space.

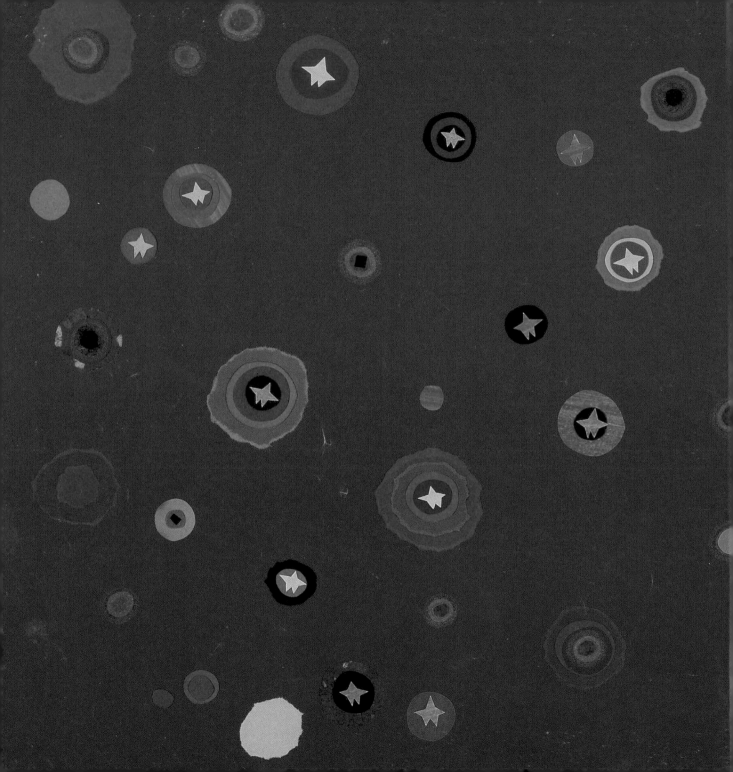